"I'M JU̲S̲T̲ ̲L̲I̲K̲E̲ ̲A̲N̲Y̲O̲N̲E̲ ̲E̲L̲S̲E̲.̲"

Premieres, parties, wardrobe changes, and photo shoots—that's what Lindsay Lohan's all about, right? Not entirely!

With four hit movies under her belt, Lindsay is one of the hottest teen actresses today, and she has no plans of slowing down anytime soon. But while Lindsay happens to be the new teen queen in Hollywood, she is also a loving daughter, a great big sister, and a loyal friend.

Confident, down-to-earth, and extremely talented, Lindsay strikes a perfect balance between being a superstar and a typical teen, which is what makes this "it" girl next door so special.

Lindsay **Lohan**

The "**It**" Girl Next Door

by Lauren Brown

Simon Spotlight
New York   London   Toronto   Sydney

For my support system:
Mom, Dad, Marc, Lindsie, Poppop, Michelle, Mindy, and Alice.
And Grandma Mickey and Grandma Molly, who I know are proud!

If you purchased this book without a cover, you should be aware that this book is stolen property. It was reported as "unsold and destroyed" to the publisher, and neither the author nor the publisher has received any payment for this "stripped book."

This book is neither authorized nor endorsed by Lindsay Lohan or any of the production companies listed herein.

SIMON SPOTLIGHT
An imprint of Simon & Schuster Children's Publishing Division
1230 Avenue of the Americas, New York, New York 10020
Text copyright © 2004 by Simon & Schuster, Inc.
All rights reserved, including the right of reproduction
in whole or in part in any form.
Designed by Chani Yammer
The text of this book was set in Berkeley Book.
SIMON SPOTLIGHT and colophon are registered
trademarks of Simon & Schuster, Inc.
Manufactured in the United States of America
First Edition 10 9 8 7 6 5 4 3 2 1
ISBN 0-689-87888-5
Library of Congress Catalog Card Number 2004109368

Table of Contents

1. A Normal Girl (Really!)	1
2. Model Behavior	10
3. Double Trouble	14
4. Back to School (with a Pit Stop in TV Land)	23
5. Freakin' Awesome	29
6. In a Huff with Hilary Duff	37
7. Confessions of a New Star	44
8. One Mean Movie	49
9. The School of Rock	59
10. The High Price of Fame	64
11. Into the Future	72
12. Lindsay's "It" List	77
13. Lindsay Gets Personal	81
14. Lindsay Goes First	88
15. Written in the Stars	92
16. We've Got Lindsay's Number	95
17. How Well Do You *Really* Know Lindsay?	99
18. Let's Go Surfing!	104

Chapter 1

•

A Normal Girl (Really!)

If Lindsay Lohan went to your school, chances are that you and she could easily become very best friends. Even though she's eighteen years old and living the glamorous life of a movie star, she's really not that different from you and your own friends at school. Lindsay loves spending time with her friends, most of whom she's known since she was a child. She's a devoted big sister to her three siblings. She loves to shop at the mall (Abercrombie & Fitch is one of her favorite stores), and her most recent crushes include Johnny Depp, Orlando

Bloom, and Colin Farrell. Sound like you and your best friends? Couldn't you easily see yourself hanging out, talking about boys, and going shopping with her? And you can probably relate to the high school characters she's played in movies like *Freaky Friday* and *Confessions of a Teenage Drama Queen*. All of Lindsay's movies have dealt with first love, friendship woes, and getting along with Mom and Dad. There's a reason for that: Lindsay only plays characters she can personally identify with. And Lindsay knows that if she has something in common with her characters, then her fans definitely do too.

No, we're not going to deny that Lindsay's face is on every magazine cover or that her movies rake in big bucks at the box office. But when she's not working (making movies and publicizing them are two very demanding and time-consuming jobs, after all), Lindsay is living the life of a normal, everyday teenager. As she told *Your Prom* magazine, "I'm just like anybody else. Just because I'm in movies or in a magazine my life's not perfect. I get up in the morning and I work hard. That doesn't make me any different."

Lindsay isn't different, but she is certainly

lucky—and busy. At eighteen, Lindsay has already starred in four hit movies (with at least four more on the way), dated a pop star (Aaron Carter), appeared in *People* magazine's "50 Most Beautiful People" issue, moved into her very own apartment with fellow actress and friend Raven, hosted the MTV Movie Awards, and recorded her first album. Most teenagers wouldn't want to be bothered with such a demanding schedule, but it's okay with Lindsay. "I have to admit, it does get exhausting. I do just want to go home and hang out with friends and stuff, but this is what I love to do," she said on the set of her hugely successful movie *Mean Girls*. "If I'm at home for a week, I'm always like, 'Okay, I need to go work now.' I can't just sit home and do nothing. I feel really blessed right now."

Even though Lindsay's life is full of glitz and glam topped with tons of hard work and demands, she still has the same worries, the same doubts, and the same fears as any normal teen. She refuses to let show business change her. Lindsay recently said during an interview on the set of *Mean Girls*, "The thing I always learn is be yourself. When you're on a movie set, you do have people doing things for you and if you need something right away, they'll be ready to do it for you. That could change people. Some people could start to get a big head from it and just think that everybody is going to always treat them like that. I think if you surround yourself with good people who will keep you in line and make sure you're not going to change, then that won't happen."

Looking back on high school, Lindsay understands the struggles girls have to go through before learning that it's always best just to be yourself. "When I was in high school, I felt like you always had to wear makeup. I was never comfortable with my skin, I hated my freckles, and I couldn't go out without base on," Lindsay reveals. "I've just gotten to be so much more comfortable with myself from being on sets. It's so much easier just to wear no makeup," she said on the *Mean Girls* set. She still sometimes struggles with being completely comfortable with her looks today (that's totally normal), but as she told *Girl's Life* magazine, she doesn't let it get her down. "My friends have that skin, that flawless, no-freckles skin. Mine is just an annoyance to me. I don't even like to lay out in the sun because I worry I'll get more freckles. But then I think, 'Suck it up and have fun.' Who wants to sit around thinking about what they don't like about their looks?" Not Lindsay.

If anything, being in the movies has given Lindsay a lot more confidence and has lessened her insecurities. When Lindsay was in high school (she went until her junior year before leaving to be homeschooled so she could concentrate on films), she didn't feel comfortable with who she was and constantly worried about her appearance. While Lindsay's long red hair and freckles have made her famous today, it took her a long time to learn to love those unique trademarks. Lindsay remembers when she was in middle school and wanted nothing more than to have the layered haircut that Jennifer Aniston made famous on *Friends*. Her mom wouldn't let her cut her long hair, but that didn't stop Lindsay from getting what she wanted. "I went to school and chopped my hair in the back of the art room," Lindsay told *People* magazine. When she got home, her mom had no choice but to take her to the hair salon. The only way her hair could be salvaged was to layer it—just like Jennifer Aniston's. Lindsay got her wish but looks back on that experience today with newfound confidence. "I love my red hair. I would never cut it," she said.

Looks aren't the only department that Lindsay stresses over from time to time. Think of the pressures at school to wear the right clothes, make good friends, and keep up with your studies. It's hard to make other people happy when you're just trying to be comfortable with yourself. Well, Lindsay has tons of pressure from agents, managers, publicists, directors, costars, and other actresses to always look good, be good, and nail the best movie roles—despite all the competition. It's a lot to deal with when you're just coming into your own. She described coping with her insecurities to Romanticmovies.com: "I have to get more confident with myself. . . . For girls my age right now, it's important that certain girls are fit and they look a certain way. You have to really get comfortable with your body. You're going to have your insecurities here and there, and I think my insecurities benefit me in a lot of ways, because [they] keep me grounded. It's just a matter of being more comfortable with yourself and growing."

Every time she goes out for roles in movies, Lindsay is constantly being compared to other girls who are incredibly talented, pretty, and successful. As she told *Seventeen* magazine, "To be in a position where you're always going to be compared to other girls near your age who are great actresses and not get horribly insecure about it or obsess about it is hard." But Lindsay has figured out how to get in the right frame of mind so the pressure doesn't drive her absolutely crazy: "There's always going to be somebody else auditioning for the same role. There's always going to be another girl who's doing the same thing as you. And if you're always going to be competitive about who's getting which roles, you're never going to be satisfied or have fun and appreciate the fact that you're doing these movies." That's a life lesson teenagers—famous or not—can relate to and apply to their own lives.

Lindsay wasn't able to attend high school full-time, but she doesn't feel like she completely missed out. She believes that the experiences and lessons she's gained from Hollywood have helped her grow up and mature, and are similar to those she would have had in high school. "I'm doing what I love to do and people are respecting me for that. In high school, you go through finding yourself. You don't really know what group you are going to hang out with. You don't really know who you're going to be when you're done with high school. Now that I'm out of high school and I've been growing up around adults most of the time, it gives you more confidence," Lindsay said during a break while filming *Mean Girls*. She definitely takes advantage of the advice she receives from adults she's worked with—especially her *Freaky Friday* costar Jamie Lee Curtis, whom she grew extremely close to during filming. Lindsay considers Jamie an important teacher and mentor. "When I worked with Jamie, we'd talk about how I tend to be very insecure, sometimes. But I think everybody does. I actually like the fact that I'm insecure, because it helps keep me grounded. I won't get ahead of myself. I think it's just working with older people that are more comfortable with themselves, you learn from them."

Lindsay is full of wit and wisdom that puts her light-years ahead of the pack. But while she can fit right in with the adults, Lindsay is still a teenager who loves to go out with her friends and have fun. She's been in love, she's had her share of crushes, and she's even had her heart broken. She loves to shop, dance, and listen to music. And like all teenagers, she admits to making her share of mistakes. When you get down to it, in a million different ways Lindsay really is just a regular teenager—just like you and your friends. You're probably excited to see what you and Lindsay have in common, so without further ado, let's get to know this girl next door a little bit better now, shall we?

Chapter 2

•

Model Behavior

On July 2, 1986, in Cold Spring Harbor, New York, Lindsay Morgan Lohan was the first of four children born to her mom, Dina, and her dad, Michael. Before long she was the proud big sister to two brothers, Michael and Dakota, and one sister, Aliana. Some say that Lindsay's fate as a star was sealed simply because she was born first—studies say that the oldest child is usually a natural born leader and high achiever. But there was more to Lindsay's fame than birth order. It was in her genes and in her heart.

Lindsay's mom, dad, and grandmother were all

seasoned veterans of the entertainment industry. Lindsay's mom was a Rockette at New York City's famous Radio City Music Hall and appeared in Broadway shows like *Cats* and *A Chorus Line*. Her dad was an actor on the soap opera *As the World Turns* when he was a child. And her grandma, Ann Valerio, was on the soap opera *Guiding Light* back when it was a radio show! The acting bug in Lindsay's family was contagious, and she couldn't wait for her turn in the spotlight.

When Lindsay was just three years old, her parents knew that her sparkling green eyes and her radiant red hair were going to make her famous. Lindsay loved singing and dancing, and she knew that she wanted to make other people laugh and clap for her. So Lindsay's parents took her to the Ford modeling agency, where she was signed as the agency's first redheaded model! Her history-making deal quickly landed her tons of jobs. And whether the world realized it or not, they were watching the future movie star Lindsay Lohan grow up in front of their eyes. Between the ages of three and eleven, Lindsay's smiling face was featured in more than sixty commercials, print ads, and other television appearances. Lindsay and her mom even got to work together when they both appeared on a show on the Family Channel called *Healthy Kids*.

Commercials were particularly fun for Lindsay to make. "My first one was for Duncan Hines," she recalled to *Girl's Life* magazine. "I remember that there was a lot of cake on the set, and all I wanted to do was eat the cake." She was in commercials for almost all of her favorite stores, restaurants, and snacks, including the Gap, Wendy's, Pizza Hut, and Jell-O (for which she appeared in a spot with Bill Cosby!). She says of the experience in *Girl's Life,* "One of my favorites was the commercial with Bill Cosby because I love to dance and I love to sing. We got to dance and sing a Jell-O song. . . . The flavor was grape. All of my friends really liked that commercial too."

When Lindsay was seven, she appeared on *Late Night with David Letterman* dressed as a piece of garbage in a skit called "Things You Find on the Bottom of the Subway." You can bet that seven-year-old Lindsay never imagined that ten years later she would be back on the show as an actual guest! Talk about surreal.

Lindsay's schedule required a lot of time from her mom, who drove her to auditions and helped

Lindsay learn her lines. More often than not, Lindsay's younger brothers and sister would have to tag along. At first it was boring for them, but eventually watching their big sister go on glamorous photo shoots and wear all kinds of fun clothes started to intrigue them. It wasn't long before they were getting in on the fun. All the Lohan kids got to appear in a Calvin Klein ad with Lindsay when they happened to be on location during the shoot. The photographer asked her siblings if they wanted to get in the shot, and it turned out so well that they used the photo in ads all over the country. You would think some big sisters would want the spotlight all to themselves, but not Lindsay. She was proud to have them all work with her.

Looking back on her modeling days, Lindsay admitted in *Teen Celebrity* magazine that it wasn't as hard being a model as people may think. "You have to travel a lot—that's the worst part. But being a model was a lot of fun." It was also the beginning of a career that would eventually put Lindsay at the top of the list of Hollywood's brightest young stars.

Chapter 3

•

Double Trouble

At eleven years old, Lindsay's career was booming. She appeared regularly in commercials, soap operas, and print ads. Balancing school and work was no problem. She would work on the soap opera *Another World* playing the role of Ali Fowler three days a week and go to school the rest of the time. Lindsay had the best of both worlds. All her acting jobs were based in New York, so she never had to be away from home. She was able to hang out with her friends at school and pursue her passion—acting.

But Lindsay knew in her heart that she wanted to

take her career to the next level: She was ready to star in a movie.

Lindsay's parents were very supportive. They weren't going to push her to act unless they knew it was exactly what she wanted to do. There are many depressing stories about parents of child actors who push their children too hard, taking the fun out of acting altogether, but Lindsay's parents were the opposite. They never even enrolled Lindsay in acting classes or hired an acting coach for her. Her mom told the *Hollywood Reporter*, "I find that acting-class kids overact. And if children are pushed into acting, it shows." So when Lindsay sent in an audition tape for the lead role in the Disney movie *The Parent Trap*, it was her natural acting abilities and her true love for performing that made her perfect for the part.

The producers at Disney received more than fifteen hundred auditon tapes from young actresses who wanted to play twin sisters Hallie and Annie. In the movie (which was a remake of the 1961 classic that starred the much-loved actress Hayley Mills), when the girls were just newborns, their parents divorced, each taking custody of one twin. The two sisters don't even know of each other's existence until they meet at summer camp.

Stepping into the shoes of an actress who some consider a legend didn't faze Lindsay a bit. She told *Daily Variety*, "I think the original *Parent Trap* is really fantastic, really good. I want to meet Miss Mills, but I don't think of [acting in] this movie as following in her footsteps."

Lindsay's confidence was a big factor in helping her land the part. Nancy Meyers, the director of *The Parent Trap*, was looking for a very special actress to play the twins. She told *USA Today*, "We weren't going to make the movie without the right kid." When the producers saw Lindsay's audition tape, they knew they were onto something amazing. "Lindsay was extremely spunky and enthusiastic," said Nancy. "She was like a little Diane Keaton." And Nancy knows a thing or two about spotting young stars. She cast a nine-year-old Drew Barrymore in the comedy-drama *Irreconcilable Differences*, a movie that showed the world that Drew was more than just "the little girl from *E.T.*" Drew would go on to become one of the most successful young women in Hollywood, with hit movies like *Charlie's Angels, The Wedding Singer,* and *50 First Dates*. Nancy could see that Lindsay had the potential to grow up to have a very similar career.

Lindsay got the call that she was one of five finalists for the dual role of Annie and Hallie, and before she knew it, she was off to Los Angeles—a city she had never visited before—for the final audition. Her entire family went with her for a whole week! During the day Lindsay—along with the other girls who were up for the part—worked with an acting coach to prepare for her last chance to impress the movie's producers, and at night she had a blast with her family at the hotel. She was completely unaware of how much her life was about to change forever.

A week later Lindsay received another phone call. This one would officially launch her career: She was going to play Hallie and Annie! Lindsay couldn't believe it. She told the *Atlanta Journal-Constitution*, "I would go to bed and pray that I could be in a movie. I just feel like my dreams have come true. I feel so lucky." Soon Lindsay and her entire family were off to London and Napa, California, where the movie would be filmed for the next three months. Her costars were Dennis Quaid (who at the time happened to be married to Meg Ryan—one of Lindsay's favorite actresses) and the Tony Award–winning actress Natasha Richardson. They would be playing her parents.

Lindsay's role was extremely demanding. Not only was she playing twins, but the girls had very different personalities . . . and accents! Annie was the prim and proper twin from London, complete with an English accent that Lindsay worked with a dialect coach to perfect. Hallie was the hip and outgoing twin from California, complete with blue nail polish on her fingers. Always up for a challenge, Lindsay had no trouble taking on two roles. "I would just keep in mind that Hallie was more spunky and Annie was the reserved one," she said in the *Atlanta Journal-Constitution*. When Lindsay's friends saw the movie, they didn't even realize that she was playing both sisters—they figured another actress played one of the twins. "They thought, 'Who's that other girl that looks just like Lindsay?' And I said, 'That girl is me!'" Lindsay told *Cinema Confidential*. "When I saw the movie, though, I noticed first about how different we were dressed but also how one girl had more freckles than the other. It was crazy how they did it."

Shooting her scenes took a lot of Lindsay's time and energy because she would often have to shoot the same scene twice in one day. In the morning she would shoot as Annie. Then it was off to change her costume and hair and then shoot the other side of the same scene as Hallie. Some of her other scenes were downright annoying to film. But no matter what the circumstance, Lindsay handled the situation like a pro. One incident that stands out in particular happened while filming the scene in which Annie loses a poker game at summer camp and has to go skinny-dipping. Lindsay somehow manages to remember the scene fondly: "I had to be in a lake late at night, and I had to stay in there for like two hours," she told the *Atlanta Journal-Constitution*. "It was sooo cold. They put this heating machine in the lake, but it didn't do much good!"

The cast and crew of *The Parent Trap* truly thought Lindsay was a natural talent for such a young actress. Charles Shyer, the film's producer, told the *Hollywood Reporter,* "Comedy is something you can't teach or explain. Lindsay just gets it. She's wise beyond her years." Nancy Meyers told the *Washington Times,* "Lindsay is such a naturally gifted actress that even the demanding stuff was kind of fun for her." And when scenes didn't go exactly right the first time, Lindsay never felt anything but encouragement. "The first time I made a mistake, the whole cast applauded and said, 'Welcome to the movie business.'"

Having her parents and siblings with her on location while she shot the movie turned it into a real family affair. Lindsay's brother Michael, who was ten at the time, was cast in a small role in the film as the only boy at the summer camp Annie and Hallie attended. The scene actually required Lindsay to fence with him. (Of course Lindsay wins!)

Lindsay's on-screen parents, Dennis Quaid and Natasha Richardson, became her extended family. They loved working with her. They saw what a tremendous amount of talent she had and tried to give her as much guidance and advice on the set as they could. Dennis told the *Hollywood Reporter,* "She's such a little pro. She knows what she's doing; she has a good work ethic; she has good manners, and she has really good natural comic talent. But she's still a little girl, which is a good thing." Dennis even gave Lindsay a gift to show her how much he enjoyed working with her—a Prada knapsack! How many eleven-year-olds carry one of those trendy bags around? As it turned out, Lindsay didn't need to receive fancy gifts, because during her downtime she was getting her fix of shopping. While shooting in London she learned about all the big designers, and when she was shooting scenes in L.A., she got a

Versace coat and a Kate Spade bag. "I get an allowance, but I usually persuade my mom to buy me things," Lindsay told the *Hollywood Reporter* while describing her newfound love of shopping.

Making *The Parent Trap* was one of the best times of Lindsay's life. While the demands of shooting a movie did get to be a bit overwhelming, Lindsay never let the pressure get to her. When she wasn't working, she was a normal kid playing with her brothers and sister. Her parents even let her have some friends come out and visit her in L.A. "We put shaving cream all over my brother and made a big mess in the hotel room," Lindsay recalled to the *Boston Herald*. "In order to get us back, he took whipped cream—it was one in the morning and my parents were sleeping—and coffee and miles of sugar and threw it on me!" Lindsay also became best friends with her stand-in. "We liked to watch videos or sit out in the sun together," Lindsay told the *Hollywood Reporter.*

Shooting her first movie flew by, and before Lindsay knew it, she was back home with her family on Long Island. While the producers and directors began editing the film and getting it ready for theaters, Lindsay went to school and settled back into life as a seventh grader. But on July 29, 1998 (the day *The Parent Trap* was released in theaters), Lindsay's life changed again. She was suddenly doing tons of press for the movie and appearing on morning talk shows like *Good Morning America* and her favorite, *The Rosie O'Donnell Show*. The movie opened to great reviews, and everyone agreed on one thing: Lindsay was a bona fide star. Lindsay could have her pick of movie roles—everyone in Hollywood was buzzing about her.

But Lindsay had other plans. She told the *Washington Times,* "I'm not gonna do another movie right away. I'm gonna be in school, stay with my family, and rest up." And she meant it.

Chapter 4

•

Back to School
(with a Pit Stop in TV Land)

The Parent Trap was a huge success, and the critics agreed that Lindsay was a talented and charming young actress. Lindsay was on her way to becoming the big-time movie star she had dreamed of being since she was a little girl. She earned a Young Artist Award for Best Leading Young Actress in a Feature Film and was nominated for both Blockbuster Entertainment and Youngstar awards. She was experiencing the kind of success after one movie that showbiz veterans work toward for years. But while Lindsay was proud of the movie and enjoying the attention she was receiving, she wasn't exactly taking meetings with her agent to plot out her next big role. Lindsay was dying to get back to school to be with her friends. She missed going to the movies and the mall, playing soccer, and skating. Lindsay wanted the next role she played to be that of a normal kid!

But Disney, the company that produced *The Parent Trap*, wasn't willing to let their new shining star go without a fight. They offered her the role of Penny in the live-action movie *Inspector Gadget*. Matthew Broderick, the comedic actor who starred as Ferris in *Ferris Bueller's Day Off*, was going to be starring in the title role. The movie sounded like it was going to be a blast to make, but in the end Lindsay decided to turn down the part. Michelle Trachtenberg (who went on to play Dawn on the television show *Buffy the Vampire Slayer*) played Penny instead.

Lindsay had no regrets. She was trying to make mature decisions about her career and the future. Part of her desire to go back to school came from lessons she was learning from her new role models. "I admire Steven Spielberg, James L. Brooks, and Jodie Foster," Lindsay told *Daily Variety*. "I like that Jodie acted, but she also knew reality and went to school."

Lindsay's attempt to have a "normal" life back at school wasn't as easy as she thought it was going to be. Thousands of people saw *The Parent Trap*. That meant Lindsay was suddenly getting recognized everywhere she went. Plus, right after the movie hit theaters, a modeling job Lindsay did for Abercrombie & Fitch led to her face being plastered on the posters in the store and on the shopping bags. Lindsay was used to being an anonymous model—after all, she had made more than sixty commercials and had hardly ever been recognized—but *The Parent Trap* changed things. "I went to the mall with my friends right after it came out," Lindsay told *Teen Celebrity*. "When we walked into Abercrombie, everyone's attention doubled and everybody was just coming up to me."

Lindsay admitted that her sudden rise to fame was a bit overwhelming, but she handled it all in stride. "I wasn't used to it at all. I had just seen it and had heard about what it was like. But now that I'm actually the one who's signing the autographs—not the one who's asking for them—it's pretty weird," she said. "It's like really a good thing to know that you mean that much to people."

Lindsay's biggest fear was that her friends would react badly to her fame. "My friends are taking this pretty well. They're definitely excited for me," she told *Good Morning America*. "I hope this doesn't change them. I hope they don't act, like, nicer to me and stuff." Lindsay had nothing to worry about. Her friends were supportive and proud of her, which confirmed that going back to school was the right decision. "My friends don't really think about it, but when they do, they're just shocked to see people come up to me and ask for my autograph," Lindsay told *BB* magazine. "They think that's so weird. I'm kind of shy with fans. If it's a little kid, I'll go up to them but I don't to just, like, show off."

After a year back at school Lindsay decided she wanted to do a few small projects just so people in show business wouldn't forget about her. Plus, acting was always her passion, and she missed it! Lindsay's pals at Disney quickly offered her a made-for-TV movie without even asking her to audition. The shoot would be much shorter than a feature-length film, so Lindsay could fit it into her school schedule. She accepted the job and was off to Vancouver to make *Life-Size* with supermodel Tyra Banks!

In *Life-Size*, Lindsay plays the starring role of Casey, a young girl grieving the death of her mother. Casey decides to cast a spell to bring her mother back to life, but she accidentally puts the spell on her doll, Eve, and Eve (played by Tyra) comes to life instead!

The character was challenging for Lindsay because, thankfully, she couldn't relate to losing a parent so early in life. "It's a really hard thing to lose your mother, and I haven't experienced that, thank God," she told *Girl's Life* magazine. "But that was one of the many things I had to realize when I was getting to know my character. I had to put all those thoughts in my head and try to become the character I was playing so I could make it as real as possible."

Lindsay loved making *Life-Size*. All of her siblings were cast as extras, and Lindsay adored working with Tyra. "It was great. I got to go to her birthday party," she told *BB* magazine. "Tyra's just normal. She's so nice." And as she mentioned to *Girl's Life* magazine, "It's not every day that you get to work with a supermodel." Working with a model was a bit challenging, though. "Tyra was so tall. She always wore sneakers when we weren't shooting," Lindsay said. "And even when she was in sneakers, I was like, 'You can't stand next to me.'"

In the end Lindsay had such a great time making the movie that going back to school and her "normal" life was a bit harder this time around.

Chapter 5

•

Freakin' Awesome

After Lindsay wrapped filming on *Life-Size*, she made one other made-for-TV movie for Disney called *Get a Clue*, in which she plays a wealthy high school student who must unravel a mystery to save one of her teachers, and she taped a TV show pilot with Bette Midler. The show was supposed to be filmed in New York, which was great because Lindsay could still go to school with her friends. But when the producers moved the show to L.A., Lindsay decided she would rather stay in the Big Apple. (It worked out for the best—the show was canceled after just one season.)

For the most part Lindsay was just an average teenager enjoying high school. But in the back of her mind she was afraid she wasn't going to be able to break back into Hollywood after taking so much time off from acting. "I started seeing other girls working more. There was drama with girls at school, and I was bored," she told *J-14*. "And I started to miss what it was like working on movies and having posters of me everywhere."

Then the audition for the lead role in Disney's remake of the classic movie *Freaky Friday* came along. Lindsay knew it was the perfect role to try out for after her three-year break. Disney remakes seemed to be a good luck charm for Lindsay. Just as the original *Parent Trap* was a career-changing film for its young star, Hayley Mills, the original *Freaky Friday* was a career-changing film for a then-teenage Jodie Foster, who went on to win two Oscars in her career!

Freaky Friday is about a girl named Anna who switches bodies with her mother after a curse is put on them. They spend an entire day living each other's lives while they try to break the spell. Experiencing what the other goes through on a daily basis brings Anna and her mother closer, and they discover a new appreciation for each other.

Lindsay had no problem landing the role of Anna, and soon her plan to go to school full-time took a backseat to the role that was about to begin her spectacular career. "When I did *Parent Trap*, I was ten. I was thrown off by the whole fame thing. It came all at once, and *Parent Trap* was an amazing movie. How do you do something that can top that? I wanted to go to school and be a normal kid," she explained to Filmforce.com. "I went to high school and I did two Disney Channel things, which were fun, just to keep up. And then *Freaky Friday* came along and it was just like, 'Wow, this is a great script and it would be perfect for me to come back with this.'"

Right after Lindsay signed on to *Freaky Friday*, things started to go a bit awry with the film. For a minute it seemed unclear if the movie would even be made at all. Actress Annette Bening, who had won a Golden Globe for her performance in *American Beauty*, was supposed to play Anna's mother. And Kelly Osbourne, reality TV's favorite bad girl, was to play her best friend and the lead singer of Anna's band. Within weeks of each other, both Annette and Kelly dropped out of the movie! Actress Jamie Lee

Curtis, who had starred in movies such as *Halloween* and *True Lies*, replaced Annette. Newcomer Christina Vidal replaced Kelly. Though at first Lindsay was disappointed, the cast changes turned out to be for the best.

While Lindsay would have loved to work with Annette Bening, Jamie Lee Curtis became a true mentor to Lindsay on the set. She gave Lindsay great advice about being an actress that Lindsay took to heart. "She's a really good person and she is really confident, but at the same time really down to earth and cool," Lindsay told Web site Tribute.ca about working with Jamie. "It's like the greatest combination, and she's everything that I want to be when I'm her age. She is so comfortable with herself, and it's so great to see that."

And while working with Kelly Osbourne probably would have been a blast, had she not left the movie Lindsay wouldn't have had the opportunity to make another one of her dreams come true: In the movie Lindsay sang a song called "Ultimate," which ended up on the film's sound track. Kelly was supposed to sing it, but when she dropped out, Lindsay confessed to the director that singing was one of her passions (in addition to acting, of course!). To complete her rocker-chick training for the role, Lindsay even learned to play the guitar for her scenes with the band. "I really wanted to learn to play—I didn't want to just fake it. Guitar is something that I've always been interested in, so when I had the chance to learn, I figured, why not take it?" she told Web site Phase9.tv. To get into rock-star mode, Lindsay even based Anna on punk rebel Avril Lavigne. "Whenever I was playing the guitar, that's who I tried to think of, just 'cause she has a coolness about her that was perfect for Anna," Lindsay said to Phase9.tv. "And girls my age can relate because Avril's someone everyone knows." *Freaky Friday* director Mark Waters was especially impressed with Lindsay's hard-rocking performance. "Lindsay is nothing like the character of Anna, who's this bad attitude, punk-rocking, tough girl—almost a tomboy," he told Romanticmovies.com. "That's not who Lindsay is, and yet, she's pulled that off brilliantly."

Just like *The Parent Trap* was a challenge for Lindsay because she had to play twins, *Freaky Friday* was difficult because she had to play a teenager *and* an adult. To get into "mom" mode, Lindsay drew inspiration from her own mother. "My mom stands a certain way and she has really good posture. So I took that from her," Lindsay told Filmforce.com. "And whenever I slouch, she goes over and she puts my back up straight. She'll probably notice that. My mom is a really cool mom. Jamie's character in the movie is very square and my mom is not very square. My mom is more like Jamie in real life."

Lindsay had a blast playing Anna because, as she told Phase9.tv, she didn't have much in common with the character. "Anna kind of keeps everything inside. Rather than saying how she feels and confiding in people, she turns to her music." Lindsay also liked the idea that seeing Anna's relationship with her mom in the film would get other girls to open up to their parents. "Girls my age hide things from their parents, and I think it's important to speak to your parents and let them know what's going on. It's like you always want what you can't have, and with teen girls, if their parents are saying they can't do certain things, they're going to want to do them more," she said on Romanticmovies.com.

Lindsay gained a newfound appreciation for her own mom while making the movie. She revealed to Phase9.tv: "I think I am my mom. We're so similar; she even looks like me—but with blonder hair. She's really cool. But I don't think I could be her for a day, because there are four kids in my family and it'd be too much work for me. I never really took the time to realize how much my mom does in a day, between getting us all to school and running around town. So it's a good movie for mothers and daughters to see together!"

So, *Freaky Friday* gave Lindsay the chance to sing, a great new mentor in Jamie Lee Curtis, and a new admiration for her mother. But another *huge* experience occurred during filming: Lindsay shared her very first on-screen kiss with heartthrob Chad Michael Murray (from hit TV shows including *Gilmore Girls, Dawson's Creek,* and *One Tree Hill*.) Lucky Lindsay, right? But smooching him in front of a room full of camerapeople was a bit more nerve-racking than she anticipated. "I talked to Chad before and I was like, 'Listen. I'm really nervous. You might not be nervous because you've done it before, but I'm really nervous. Just know that,'" Lindsay told Phase9.tv. "We shot that scene for two days straight. He's really good looking, so it wasn't bad, you know what I mean? I know a lot of girls who are obsessed with Chad, so that was a huge plus for me. And he's really sweet, too."

Freaky Friday made more than one hundred

million dollars at the box office, and both Lindsay and Jamie received rave reviews. Surprisingly, this was something that neither of them expected! "The whole time Jamie and I were filming, we kept saying we were going to suck. But when the movie hit one hundred million, Jamie made us T-shirts that said 'We didn't suck.'" In fact, Jamie was nominated for a Golden Globe for her performance!

Jamie made sure she gave Lindsay tons of great advice and helped her keep a level head about her new success. In the *Los Angeles Times* Jamie said, "I told Lindsay, 'This does not happen a lot. If it does, it's alchemy.'" That was for sure. All signs started pointing to superstardom for Lindsay.

Chapter 6

In a Huff with Hilary Duff

One of the hardest things about being thrust into the public eye as a result of your success is the media attention you get. Sometimes the press looks for other people in similar situations to pit against you to create a "rivalry." Remember when Christina Aguilera came on the scene almost immediately after Britney Spears? Because Christina was a blonde and sang pop music, she was compared to Britney. And in the blink of an eye, those comparisons turned into rumors that Britney and Christina were bitter enemies and hated each other. After all, rumors like these make for great gossip and tabloid fodder.

Well, the same thing happened with Lindsay and fellow actress Hilary Duff. Before Lindsay starred in *Freaky Friday* and started to get major buzz in Hollywood, Hilary was the "it" girl. She was starring in the hit Disney sitcom *Lizzie McGuire* and had two big movies under her belt, including *Agent Cody Banks* and a big-screen version of *Lizzie McGuire*. Like Lindsay, Hilary loved to sing, and in 2003 she released an album called *Metamorphosis*. Lindsay knew the comparisons with Hilary were inevitable, and commented on it to *Twist* magazine: "When you're acting and you're around girls your age, everybody wants to be like each other." And it wasn't that Hilary and Lindsay necessarily tried to be like each other—they felt that they were planning out very different career paths. But they just couldn't help their similarities, and the press couldn't help but pick up on them. They both were fresh-faced actresses with the same young fan base. They were up for many of the same roles, and they both sang. Soon, it seemed, these similarities evolved into a full-fledged rivalry. Rumors flew that the girls couldn't stand each other or bear being in the same room together. What started out as some friendly competition appeared to slowly turn into animosity . . . and it wasn't pretty!

So what happened? Well, as much as we hate to say it, Lindsay and Hilary started feuding with each other over a boy.

Around the time she was filming *Freaky Friday*, Lindsay began dating pop star Aaron Carter. She was sixteen and busy pursuing her acting career, and he was fifteen and focusing on his music career.

And then Lindsay found out that Aaron was in a relationship with none other than Hilary Duff.

It's hard enough to confront a boyfriend when you're having problems of this magnitude. But when there is a chance that the press could find out about your problems and write all about them for tons of people to read? That would be a downright nightmare. So when Lindsay and Hilary (and their thousands of fans) discovered they had yet another thing in common—the same pop star boyfriend—things turned ugly.

Lindsay and Hilary's feud over Aaron was something out of the halls of any high school in America. Lindsay told the *Los Angeles Times* that one of Hilary's friends left a message on Lindsay's answering machine saying that she was "fat and needed to do Pilates." (Seriously, girls can be so cruel.) Then rotten eggs were thrown on Hilary's Range Rover, and someone told Hilary's mom that Lindsay was to blame. (Lindsay was apparently not even in town at the time.) Suddenly the girls couldn't even be at the same events together. Lindsay told *Good Morning America*, "My thing with Hilary is a high school thing. It's the reason why I wanted to finish school early. When you are working, the last thing you want to read is someone doesn't like you. Let it go." As for Hilary's side of the story, she thought that Aaron and Lindsay's relationship was over when she started dating him! "He made it look like they had broken up," Hilary told *Twist* magazine. "I think Aaron cheated on me and I think he cheated on Lindsay."

Even if that were the case, the girls still didn't see eye to eye. In the spring of 2003, Lindsay and Hilary were invited to appear on the cover of *Vanity Fair* as part of a special issue devoted to young, up-and-coming teen stars. Mary-Kate and Ashley Olsen, Amanda Bynes, Raven, and Mandy Moore were some of the other stars featured, and everyone involved was extremely honored to be part of the article. But it was obvious that all of the young Hollywood stars were also excited to learn whether the rumors of Lindsay and Hilary's feud were true. They couldn't wait to see how the two girls would treat each other.

But no one was quite prepared for what ended up happening.

When Hilary showed up at the shoot, she wasn't alone. She had Aaron on her arm! Lindsay was very uncomfortable with the situation and didn't think she could do her best work if Aaron was there, so she asked the representatives from *Vanity Fair* if they could please ask Aaron to leave. They agreed, which upset Hilary and caused a scene (complete with Hilary breaking down in tears). Tensions were running high, but this battle was just the beginning of a major war between Hilary and Lindsay.

A few months later, at the premiere party for Lindsay's movie *Freaky Friday*, Hilary showed up with Lindsay's costar Chad Michael Murray. Hilary and Chad were good friends because they had just started filming *A Cinderella Story* together. But this was Lindsay's first big premiere since *The Parent Trap* and the celebration meant a lot to her. It was unfortunate for Lindsay that of all the girls in Hollywood, Chad had chosen to ask Hilary to be his date.

Fast-forward four months to the premiere of

Hilary's movie *Cheaper by the Dozen*. Twentieth Century Fox, the studio behind *Cheaper by the Dozen,* invited Lindsay to attend. She decided to go—and *not* as a way to get back at Hilary for coming to the *Freaky Friday* premiere! If Lindsay and Hilary were both going to be working in this business, they were going to have to prove that they could attend events together as civil young adults. But according to some reports, Hilary and her mom, Susan, were not pleased when they saw Lindsay arrive at the party. Susan even went as far as trying to get a bodyguard to throw Lindsay out. Sounds like something out of a movie, right? But this was real life! Executives from Twentieth Century Fox insisted that Lindsay stay—after all, she had been invited as a guest of the studio—and Lindsay partied the night away with the other stars of *Cheaper by the Dozen*, including hottie Ashton Kutcher. Instead Hilary and her mom left the party and later said their departure had nothing to do with Lindsay; Hilary had an early flight to Boston the next day.

When news about the *Cheaper by the Dozen* premiere was reported in the media, Lindsay was fed up. She was getting tired of having to constantly comment on her feud with Hilary to the press. Lindsay told *J-14,* "I have no problem with Hilary. Maybe she has a problem with me, but I don't think that she should. She doesn't need to do that. Her career is going great. Her CD is doing well. But I don't think it helps getting people kicked out of premieres. I wish her the best of luck. If my mom got involved with something, I'd be very embarrassed."

The drama has since died down, and Lindsay has made it clear to the press that there is no need for them to harp on it anymore. "No, I don't hate Hilary," she told *Seventeen* magazine. "We're friends with the same people. I'd have no friends right now if I hated her and all of her friends." And when Lindsay was a guest on MTV's *Total Request Live,* she was asked to send a message to anyone she chose. What did she say? "I love you, Hilary Duff." Sure, it was a little sarcastic, but definitely a step in the right direction.

Chapter 7

Confessions of a New Star

The summer of 2003 was overwhelming for Lindsay, yet one of the best times of her life. She promoted *Freaky Friday* and enjoyed the perks of fame and all of the critical praise that was being heaped on her. When she was asked to appear in the *Vanity Fair* teen stars issue mentioned earlier, it was proof that she had really arrived at stardom. She couldn't believe her luck.

When Lindsay's fans from *The Parent Trap* days realized that the teenager in the movie posters for *Freaky Friday* was the same adorable, freckle-faced actress all grown up, Lindsay's fame instantly doubled. "I was walking past Mel's Diner and there were these little girls outside, and the billboard [for *Freaky Friday*] was right across the street," she told Romanticmovies.com. "So everyone started looking, and this little girl started whispering, 'My God, that's Lindsay Lohan!'"

As Lindsay adjusted to fame, she made sure she stayed grounded. "I don't think I have personally changed, and my friends haven't changed, but people do recognize me more sometimes than they would have before *Freaky Friday*, and that's a great feeling," she told Tribute.ca. "I feel really honored to be able to be doing this and for people to be enjoying it. I just want to keep doing it as long as I can." Lindsay also kept the advice she received from Jamie Lee Curtis in the back of her head. "She just said, 'Make sure you're just having fun, because it's a lot of work and it can get stressful and you get to a point where a lot of stuff is going on and it gets to you, and you just have to make sure you're around good people.'"

When Lindsay finished promoting *Freaky Friday* she joined the fantastic cast and crew of her next movie, *Confessions of a Teenage Drama Queen*. This was yet another project with Disney, and the role was Lindsay's most demanding character yet. She plays Lola, an aspiring actress from New York City whose family moves to the suburbs of New Jersey. The popular girls at her new school don't exactly appreciate Lola's crazy stories, wild wardrobe, or obsession with the rock band Sidarthur. But they get especially upset when Lola lands the coveted lead role in the school play. Veteran actress Carol Kane plays Lola's eccentric and slightly neurotic drama teacher, and Alison Pill plays her new best friend Ella, whom Lola manages to bring out of her shell when the two of them head to New York City to see Sidarthur play their final concert.

When Lindsay read the script, she knew she was perfect for the role. "It has a really cute message, kind of a 'believe in yourself' type of thing. It's very relatable, and I think that's important at my age with my audience," Lindsay told MTV.com. "I'd like to stick with my audience for as long as I can, 'cause when you go forward, you can't really go back. If I can do something that's positive for younger kids—even girls my age—that's cute and fun, I might as well do it while I can."

Lindsay had a blast playing Lola. She had a lot

in common with her character—they both had to balance the demands of an acting career and school. "She's kind of eccentric in her own way because she's into doing what she wants to accomplish in life," Lindsay told Romanticmovies.com. "She's trying to believe in herself and accomplish her goals."

And since the movie was about a drama queen, the entire film was filled with outrageous costumes, crazy dream sequences, and elaborate dance numbers. "It was a lot of work, but it was a different kind of work because it was different from acting every single day," she told Romanticmovies.com. "We had great people working with us. We had a great musical producer, we had a great musical supervisor, and we had a great choreographer, so it was more fun than anything else for me." Lindsay had more than forty costume changes throughout the movie and she loved every last skirt, dress, and shoe. "It keeps your energy up, instead of 'this outfit again?' It was fun. It was a lot of fun," she explained to Tribute.ca. And it turns out that Lindsay could relate to the whole drama queen idea: "I look back and I hate how I was in the seventh grade. I was so into pleasing everyone and dressing a certain way," she told Phase9.tv. "It was just like a huge fashion thing back then, because at my school it was grades seven through twelve, so we were in school with seniors and that was very intimidating. You tend to grow up really fast when you're around older kids, and I definitely went through a drama queen phase. I'm still going through it!"

While Lindsay played a drama queen in the movies she was enjoying royalty in real life, too. Lindsay had been officially crowned the new queen of the teen stars.

Chapter 8

•

One Mean Movie

Right after Lindsay turned seventeen, she made one of the most important decisions of her entire life. Realizing that if she wanted her career to keep growing she needed to be as close to Hollywood as possible, she announced that she was going to leave her family in New York and move to Los Angeles—on her own.

Neither of Lindsay's parents could move to California with her, because they had jobs on the East Coast and three children to take care of, so at first Lindsay's mom was more than a little nervous about one of her "babies" living on her own all the way across the country. "My parents went through this withdrawal phase when I told them. They were like, 'You're not going to be living there full-time, right? You are going to be back and forth?'" Lindsay said on the set of *Mean Girls*. "My mom was so afraid that I was going move out and never talk to them again!"

Lindsay's parents finally accepted her decision. They knew that Lindsay was mature and responsible enough to handle living away from home, and they understood that if Lindsay wanted to audition for the best movie roles she needed to be in Hollywood. But they weren't willing to let her go off to L.A. completely unsupervised (Lindsay still was a minor, after all). So they found a guardian who would accompany Lindsay to work and make sure that she was taking care of herself. But this guardian wouldn't be living with Lindsay—just checking in and chaperoning her as needed. Lindsay would be moving into her very first apartment with her new friend and fellow actress Raven, who was best known as three-year-old Olivia on the *Cosby Show* before she grew up to star in the Disney Channel sitcom *That's So Raven*. The two roommates actually met at the *Vanity Fair* shoot!

"Raven's really cool. She's really honest, and I like that. She's mature and she's grown up around adults, like me, so we'll mesh well," Lindsay told *Girl's Life* magazine.

Lindsay and Raven's first decision as roommates was what size apartment they should move into. Since neither of them were going to be home very much due to their crazy work schedules, a big apartment didn't seem to make sense to Raven. But Lindsay disagreed. "At first, Raven didn't want to get the bigger apartment because she didn't want to have people over all the time. But I was like, 'First of all, we need the bigger apartment because I can't fit anything in the closet!' The closet is too small in the smaller apartment. And I need to have people over. I don't like being home alone," Lindsay explained on the set of *Mean Girls*.

The next thing on the new roommates' agenda was decorating. Thankfully Raven was into details, because Lindsay had no desire to worry about things like paint colors for the bathroom or furniture for the den. "I was out in L.A. for three days before we moved in, and Raven was like, 'Okay, we need to get paint and bedroom sets and do this and that.' I was like, 'Yeah, I'm not in the mood to do that now.' So she got paint and really handled everything. She's like very ahead of herself. She's been very mature and very organized with moving into the apartment. I think that's good and I think that's why we get along so well," Lindsay said on the *Mean Girls* set. (It turns out that letting Raven handle the decorating was a good idea. Lindsay was so busy shooting movies that she was rarely at home, and in August 2004 Lindsay and Raven moved into separate L.A. pads.)

The girls finally got their apartment in order, but before Lindsay could officially settle in she was whisked away to Toronto to star in the movie *Mean Girls*. The script was written by *Saturday Night Live* star Tina Fey (the show's hilarious "Weekend Update" anchor and *SNL*'s first female head writer—ever). Tina's script was adapted from Rosalind Wiseman's book *Queen Bees & Wannabes: Helping Your Daughter Survive Cliques, Gossip, Boyfriends & Other Realities of Adolescence*, a nonfiction account of the harsh realities girls face in high school, such as betrayal from friends, nasty rumors, and backstabbing. Tina appeared in the movie as an algebra teacher who shows the girls that mean and nasty isn't the best way to play. Other *SNL* actors—both past and present—also starred, including Amy Poehler (as the mother of the most popular girl in school), Tim Meadows (as the principal), and Ana Gasteyer (as Lindsay's character's mom). Working with them was a thrill for Lindsay and the other young cast members who grew up watching *SNL*. "They're so funny and they bring so much to the script and so much to the characters. It's so amazing to be around them," Lindsay told MTV.com.

The rest of the cast included Lacey Chabert from *Party of Five*; Rachel McAdams, who starred in *The Hot Chick*; and Jonathan Bennett, who plays Lindsay's very cute love interest. And Lindsay was thrilled that the movie was helmed by her *Freaky Friday* director, Mark Waters, with whom she already had a great relationship.

In *Mean Girls*, Lindsay plays a girl named Cady who lives in the jungle with her zoologist parents until they move back to the suburbs and enroll Cady in public school for the first time ever at age sixteen. Cady quickly discovers that high school is really just a different kind of jungle. She instantly makes friends with Damian and Janis, members of the "out crowd." Then she meets the Plastics, the three most beautiful, popular girls in school, who immediately invite Cady into their group. Cady soon falls for the ex-boyfriend of the head Plastic, Regina. In typical mean girl fashion, when Regina finds out, she starts dating him again, prompting Cady to plot with Damian and Janis to bring the Plastics down. But in order to do that, Cady has to pretend she's one of them!

Originally Lindsay wanted to play head mean girl, Regina. But in the end Lindsay got her mean girl fix, since there are several scenes in the movie in which Cady is less than sweet. As she told *Seventeen* magazine, "I wanted to play the mean girl to just do something different. But I don't want my audience to think I'm actually mean." As if! It was clear that Lindsay was having a blast, which she admitted to the *Winnipeg Sun*: "It was so much fun [to be mean in the movie]. I've never got to do that before. I went to public school until my senior year, which I took at home and with tutors, so I know all about school cliques. According to the hierarchy in the book *Queen Bees & Wannabes*, I was a floater in real life. I got along with most people because I was a jock, a cheerleader, and was into arts and music. I could successfully go from one group to another. I never had that feeling of being ostracized, which is what *Mean Girls* is all about."

Filming *Mean Girls* made Lindsay reflect on her own experiences in high school. She wanted the movie to entertain her fans, but she also hoped it would make real-life mean girls think twice. "I think in high school you're under a lot of pressure to be like something you may not be, act a certain way, or do certain things," Lindsay said on the movie set. "For me, it was difficult because people thought I was a certain way because I was an actress. They never really got to know me because I was never really there. I think it's just important in high school to just be yourself and surround yourself with friends that you can trust." Lindsay didn't necessarily agree with the way Cady goes back and forth between the popular and unpopular groups at school. "I think she loses herself in the process of being other girls and being something she's not. At one point in the movie, Cady's personality changes, and it's not for the better," she said.

Cady's personality changes also meant big-time wardrobe changes for Lindsay. "Cady goes from wearing earth tones, in, like, cargo pants and work boots, to dressing in mini-skirts and stilettos! It's always fun to dress like that. I hate the days we filmed that I had to dress dowdy, because it's not fun, and all the other girls are really hot on set, and you're like, 'Ugggh!'" she said during filming. "There was one outfit that I had to wear that was like nothing. It was a piece of fabric that was supposed to be a dress. I was like all dolled up because it's supposed to show a drastic change. I had on all this makeup and black eyeliner. It was fun but I felt so overdone!"

Starring in a movie that takes place in high school can often turn into a mini version of the real thing with so many young actors and actresses on the set. But everyone got along really well during shooting. Lindsay was a little worried about how she would get along off-screen with Jonathan, since she knew from past experience that filming kissing scenes could make things weird, but it turned out that Lindsay had nothing to worry about. "Jonathan and I get along really well. It's always awkward when you're working with a guy who you have to be attracted to on set, because you start to like them. Stuff like that always happens at my age. But we get along really well and it's on a good, professional level," she explained during shooting.

Lindsay was also nervous that, with so many up-and-coming actresses in the movie, egos would get in the way—but that was definitely not the case. "It's not too often that you get a bunch of girls together in a room and get along so well. We all have fun together and we hang when we're not shooting, too," Lindsay said. Lindsay hasn't always found that kind of camaraderie on past movie sets with her peers, so she knew it was rare and that she was lucky. "When you're acting and you're around girls your own age who all want to act and go after the same roles as you, it's hard not to be competitive. You're never going to be happy or satisfied until you realize that you just have to deal with it because there is always going to be somebody doing something similar to you. I am the same person on set that I am at home with my friends."

Making *Mean Girls* was a big stepping stone in Lindsay's career. She earned a million-dollar paycheck, and the film opened at number one at the box office. Plus, it was the first time Lindsay felt like a leader among her peers. "When I was doing *Freaky Friday* and *The Parent Trap*, I had adult actors that I could turn to if I needed anything. Now it's different. With *Mean Girls*, I'm number one on the call sheet," Lindsay said during filming. "I had a talk with Mark and he was like, 'You know, there's no Jamie [Lee Curtis] on this set. You have to hold your own and be the responsible one and let people look up to you.' That scared me a bit because if I do mess up here and there, I don't want people to think I'm immature on the set and stuff."

No one thought Lindsay was anything but a true professional. And fans who watched Lindsay in *The Parent Trap* or *Freaky Friday* got to see the most mature side of Lindsay's acting abilities to date. Starring in an edgier and slightly older movie was a big reason Lindsay signed on to *Mean Girls*. "It's fun to change and it's more fun to play a character who goes through a transformation than to play someone who's static, because you don't get to experience both and you don't get to show a change in the character and you're just playing one person the whole time," Lindsay said during filming. Her more experienced costars in the film—including Tina Fey—were highly impressed with Lindsay. "I would watch Lindsay to learn what it is to be a film actor," Fey told *People*. "At the same time, Lindsay really was a teenager. She'd be on her pink cell phone calling her mom or online trying to track down baby-blue Uggs."

© 2004 Getty Images

Greeting fans with her *Freaky Friday* costar Jamie Lee Curtis

Not-so-mean girls: Lindsay with Tina Fey

All smiles at the premiere of *Cheaper by the Dozen*

A fan favorite at Nickelodeon's Kids' Choice Awards 2004

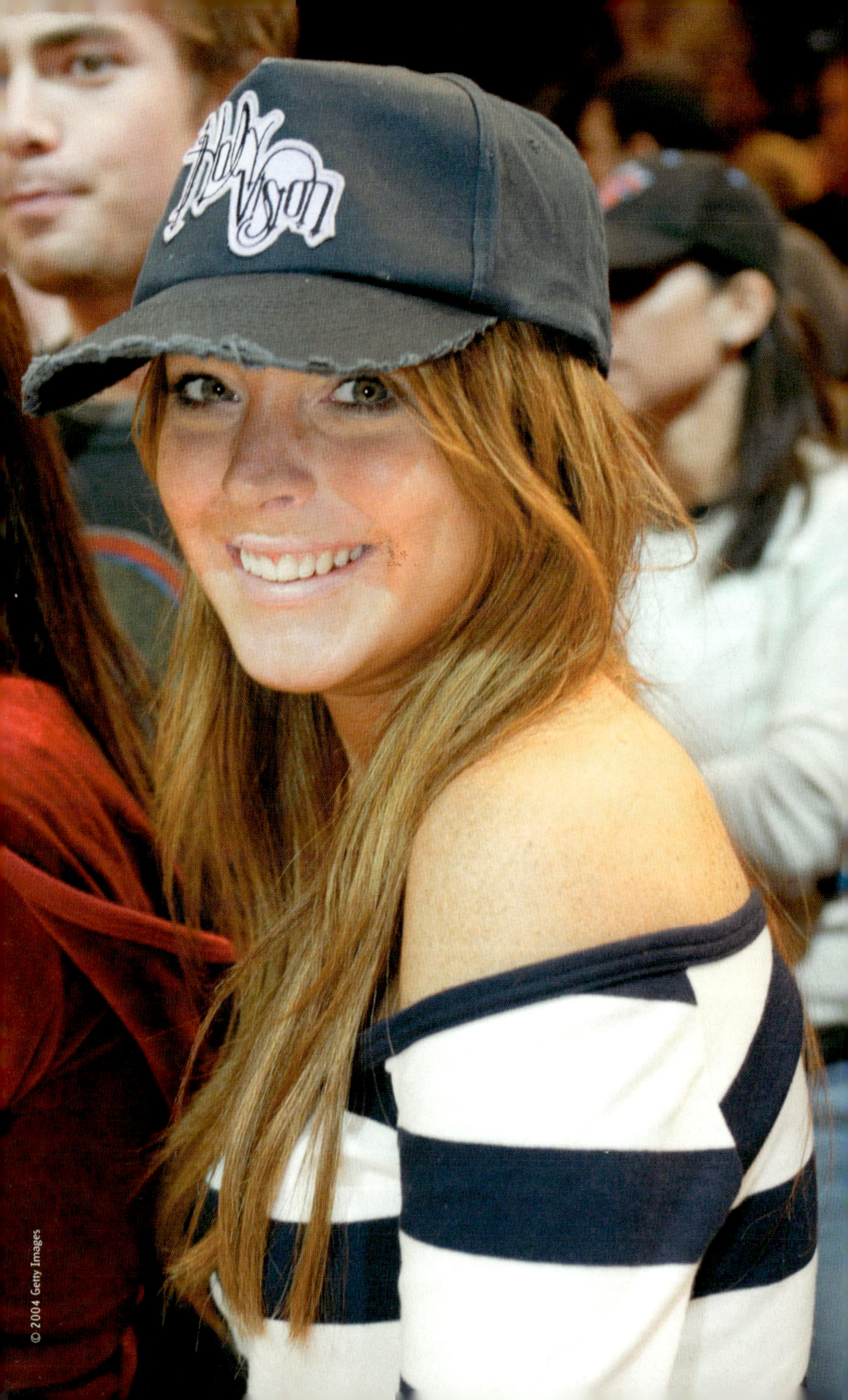

Out and about with Raven!

Sharing a laugh with little brother Dakota

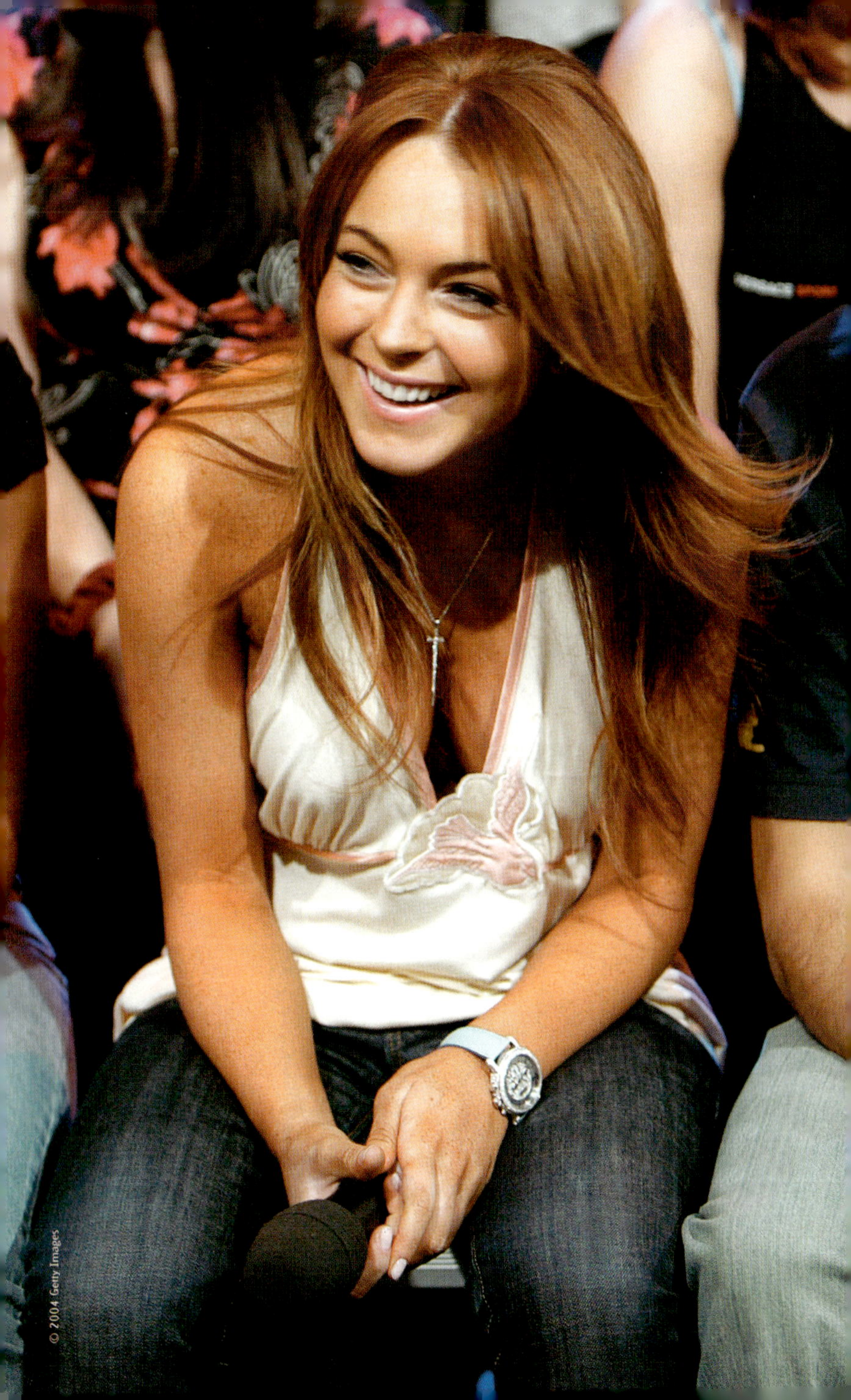

Hanging out at MTV with fellow "it" stars actress Kate Bosworth, snowboarder Shaun White, and singer Fefe Dobson

Looking like a rock star at the 2003 MTV Video Music Awards

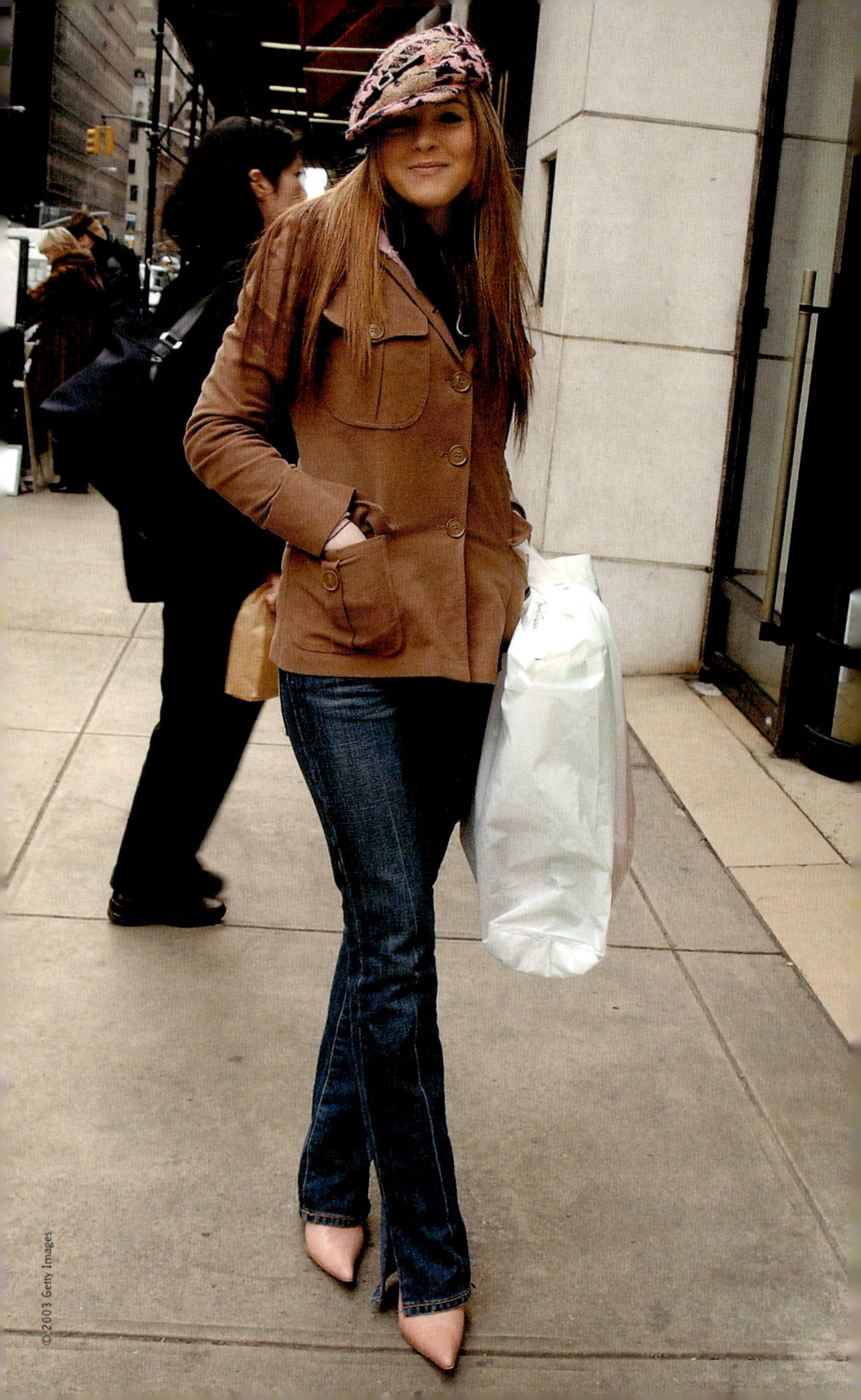

Chapter 9

The School of Rock

It was no coincidence that Lindsay sang in both *Freaky Friday* and *Confessions of a Teenage Drama Queen*. As much as Lindsay loves acting, she's always had a major passion for singing, as well. But Lindsay was nervous about balancing an acting career *and* a singing career, and she wasn't entirely sure if she wanted to do both. Plus, since she was so successful in her acting, she was okay with waiting for the right time to sing. Lindsay told *J-14* magazine, "I've been singing almost as long as I've been acting. I don't want people to think I'm an actress trying to sing."

She considered opportunities that would have allowed her to both act and sing; before she landed the role in *Freaky Friday*, Lindsay thought about starring in a Broadway show. "I met with the people who were casting for *Gypsy* on Broadway," she told *J-14*. "That was something that I was really interested in, but *Freaky Friday* started at the same time as rehearsals, so it didn't work out."

So instead Lindsay subtly worked some singing into her movies. She sang "Ultimate" on the *Freaky Friday* sound track. She also sang a few songs for the *Confessions of a Teenage Drama Queen* sound track, including "Drama Queen (That Girl)" and a medley that included a cover of the David Bowie song "Changes." "Music is a big part of my life. If I'm upset and driving in my car, I'll put slow music on. If I'm mad, I'll listen to something crazy," she told *J-14* magazine.

After *Freaky Friday*, two things kept Lindsay out of the recording studio. Number one: She was filming back-to-back movies. That didn't exactly leave a lot of free time. And number two: Hilary Duff released her debut album, *Metamorphosis*, in August 2003 after contributing songs to *her* films' sound tracks. Lindsay was already fighting off comparisons to Hilary on a daily basis, so she decided to hold off and wait for the right time to start her own music career. Lindsay told Filmforce.com, "I've always been interested in singing, and I've always been singing and dancing since I was little. It's hard right now because I don't want to just be one in the pack. I want to separate myself."

Finally Lindsay, who writes song lyrics in her journal whenever she gets a free moment, decided that she wanted to start recording music that had nothing to do with her movies.

After wrapping *Mean Girls,* Lindsay had some free time in her schedule, so she decided to head into the studio and record a few songs just for fun. She loved the idea of recording without the pressure of a record label. That way, she could experiment with all different kinds of music and producers and not feel the stress of walking away with a completed project. If Lindsay liked what she recorded, then she would weigh her options. Lindsay said to Filmforce.com, "I don't know exactly what I'm gonna do yet. I don't want to stay away from anything, though I probably won't be singing country, I know that. That's not my fan base. I see myself doing hip-hop beats with a guitar. I want to be edgy."

So, filled with confidence and excitement, Lindsay officially went into the recording studio in the spring of 2004. She invited famous music industry experts to join her in the studio, including producer Randy Jackson, the judge from *American Idol*, and Grammy-winning songwriter Diane Warren (who wrote the Aerosmith hit "I Don't Wanna Miss a Thing"). And in July 2004 Lindsay inked a deal with Tommy Mottola's Casablanca Records. Mottola, who helped make Mariah Carey and Jennifer Lopez into superstars, told the *New York Post*, "I'm thrilled we have [Lindsay]. I think she's the next big star on the horizon." The album should be finished by the end of 2004!

The help Lindsay received in the studio was amazing, but she really wants to take control of her music as much as possible. She told MTV.com, "I write a lot of lyrics and I'm involved in the producing process, because it's like, if I'm singing it, I want it to be something that I can relate to. I'm just trying to feel it out and see where it goes." Lindsay also contributed to her songs instrumentally by playing guitar!

When the record is complete, Lindsay wants to take time off from acting. "I really enjoy singing and

I really enjoy acting, [but] singing I've been doing since I was really young," Lindsay told MTV.com. "It's just about finding the right material and the right kind of vibe that I want to go with. And I want to focus on my music career; I don't want to just do it and then toss it aside. I don't want people to be like, 'Oh, she thinks she can sing 'cause she is, like, in movies and stuff.'" It seems unlikely that Lindsay will ever have that problem. When you believe in something the way Lindsay believes in her music, people appreciate that and respect you even more as a result!

As far as her music career is concerned, Lindsay says that her real dream come true would be working with the Neptunes (Pharrell Williams's producing team). Also, at some point she would love to collaborate with her idols, Madonna and Janet Jackson. But Lindsay's realistic that those pairings may not happen for a while. "That would be awesome, but I gotta get my own stuff out first," Lindsay told MTV.com.

Chapter 10

•

The High Price of Fame

After the phenomenal success of *Mean Girls*, Lindsay's career skyrocketed. She was officially the new "it" girl in town, and fans all over the world could not get enough of her.

In May 2004 Lindsay hosted *Saturday Night Live*, a prestigious honor that very few seventeen-year-olds ever get asked to do. Some wondered if Lindsay was ready for such a high-profile job, but she proved them wrong with her dead-on impressions and wit throughout the night. During her opening monologue, she even poked fun at her feud with Hilary

Duff! (Although, Hilary was not so amused. After watching the skit, she told *Us Weekly*, "It's mean when they make fun of people like that.")

Lindsay became an instant media favorite. She graced the covers of magazines like *Seventeen* and *Interview*. She was named one of *People*'s 50 Most Beautiful People of 2004. She also found out that she was nominated for an MTV Movie Award in the Breakout Female category for her performance in *Freaky Friday* (which she would go on to win), placing her in the company of other critically acclaimed young actresses such as Evan Rachel Wood, Scarlett Johansson, and Keira Knightley. Lindsay was on cloud nine.

And then came the opportunity of a lifetime: Lindsay was offered the chance to follow in the footsteps of major stars like Sarah Michelle Gellar, Jack Black, Justin Timberlake, and Seann William Scott and actually *host* the 2004 MTV Movie Awards. Everything that Lindsay had worked so hard for since she was a child was coming together!

But, as Lindsay has learned, with a high level of success comes a high level of scrutiny from the press. Once again Lindsay's every move was watched, analyzed, exaggerated, and written about—including plenty of false information. Lindsay told *J-14,* "You have reporters writing about you and everyone believes what they read. You have to brush it off. If you let it get to you, you'll never be happy." Lindsay is an old pro at dealing with the press, especially after fighting off the tabloids during her feud with Hilary Duff. Besides, she was too excited to let the tabloids get her down.

However, Lindsay may not have been quite prepared for the kind of attention that she started to get from the media and even her fans at this white-hot point in her career. For starters, Lindsay had the scare of her life when a man started stalking her whenever she was out with her friends. Things got out of hand when Lindsay was at a birthday bash for one of her friends and this same man tried to crash the party. After the bouncers wouldn't let him in, he lied to the police and told them that Lindsay was inside drinking. Seeing as Lindsay is too young to drink and way too responsible to break the law, it just shows what lengths creeps will go to in order to intrude in Lindsay's life.

But aggressive fans were just the beginning.

Like every teenager, Lindsay loves going out with her friends and having a good time. But because

Lindsay is a workaholic, she doesn't get to go out as much as she would like. So when Lindsay does have time off, there is nothing she'd rather do than blow off some steam with her friends. Unfortunately, these days, wherever Lindsay goes the press goes too. Sometimes reporters assume that because she's a young, famous, successful movie star she has to be partying hard and causing trouble in some way, which isn't exactly fair! Especially since in reality Lindsay has a strong sense of right and wrong. She told *Seventeen* magazine, "When my friends and I go out, we just get a table and observe what goes on. We're calm. We know our place. We don't have to get stupid and drunk—we can have fun without drinking. You're not supposed to drink in clubs till you're twenty-one, so we have Red Bulls."

The media's sudden obsession with Lindsay is especially hard for her to deal with because she knows she has an image to maintain for her young fans. Plus, because she makes so many movies for Disney, she is expected to uphold their wholesome standards at all times. "Disney is very protective of our relationship. It's kind of like old Hollywood—they kind of guide your career," Lindsay explained in *Seventeen* magazine. "So it's hard to see the Mischas

[Barton from *The O.C.*] and the other girls who can go out and get away with things." Lindsay knows what her fans expect of her and she tries to live up to those expectations. It's not easy when every week a different tabloid prints a new story about Lindsay doing something bad, but she tries to ignore it and continues to go out. "I don't want to have a drink and have someone whip out a camera phone and Disney getting [a picture of] it. It's not worth it. I don't want to risk my career for a night of having fun," she said in *Seventeen*. "Everyone looks at you under a microscope."

Lindsay has a plan to get the press off her back, but it hasn't exactly been easy to put into action: "I think the best thing for someone my age, the thing that I need right now, just to keep me grounded, is a boyfriend," Lindsay told *Seventeen* magazine. "Just because going out a lot gives people the wrong impression about you, and if you have a boyfriend you have a reason to stay home a lot, and you have someone to talk to. The thing that's hard is that when you're looking for a boyfriend, when you're looking for someone, you're not going to find them."

Another setback Lindsay has experienced is that guys sometimes find her intimidating. "I think it's because I'm very honest. I always speak my mind; like if you're bothering me or doing something that's offensive to me, I'm going to tell you rather than talk about you behind your back. But if I don't know you yet, I can be very shy," she told *YM* magazine.

Lindsay knows that a boyfriend isn't the key to happiness. But because the paparazzi insists on documenting her life, it puts her dating life under the microscope too, which makes finding Mr. Right a challenge. Any guy Lindsay chats with, meets at an event, or is introduced to—especially when the guy happens to be another celebrity—instantly becomes her "boyfriend" in the tabloids and the situation gets blown out of proportion. "Recently they wrote something about Colin Farrell and me that wasn't true," Lindsay told *Teen People*. "I met him only once at *Live with Regis and Kelly*!"

The press also linked Lindsay with Wilmer Valderrama (Fez from *That '70s Show*). This time, it appears the media was more on target! After she turned eighteen in July 2004, Lindsay and Wilmer stopped denying that they are an item. Wilmer's age—he's twenty-four—isn't a problem for Lindsay. She admitted to *YM* that she's attracted to older guys. "It's easier for me, maturity wise, to talk to them. But it's not like I'm going to date a thirty-year-old—unless it's Jude Law. My parents and I have an agreement that dating him would be okay!"

Lindsay has managed to keep a good attitude about the overwhelming amount of media coverage she's been getting lately. Instead of hiding out or putting her life on hold, she's looking at it as a chance to find herself. "I'm learning, and I'd rather make my own mistakes and learn from them than have to be sheltered my whole life," Lindsay said in *People* magazine. Lindsay's good friend Jaime Gleicher, who starred in MTV's reality show *Rich Girls*, told *People*, "To call Lindsay a saint wouldn't be fair to her. She knows she's not a saint. But she's not as wild as people think. If there's anything Lindsay does in excess, it's dance. She loves to dance." With that said, you can understand Lindsay's shock when she turned up on the cover of *Us Weekly* with the headline "Teens Gone Wild." Lindsay explained to the *Los Angeles Times*, "It's hard being seventeen years old and not be able to do the same things that other seventeen-year-olds do."

Lindsay has accepted that every time she goes out with her friends there is a chance the tabloids will make it look like she is up to no good. But Lindsay could never have imagined that the normal, everyday things she did in broad daylight would get twisted into a huge ordeal by the press. "I had my first fender bender not too long ago, and someone I thought was my friend reported it to *Us Weekly* and made up all these lies about what I did. My first accident ever! I was going to a meeting at three in the afternoon and they made it look like it was three in the morning," she told *Seventeen* magazine.

While Lindsay may seem fed up, she is mature enough to simply acknowledge that all the attention is part of being in the public eye. Lindsay told *Interview* magazine, "They're [the paparazzi] just doing their job. For me to go, 'Oh, my God, they're so annoying,' would be obnoxious and unfair. I mean, I kind of asked for all that when I got into this business. It's just upsetting when people start making things up."

Chapter 11

Into the Future

After the amazing couple of years that Lindsay's had, it doesn't take a crystal ball to forecast that her future will be nothing but bright! She has six movies on the way, a record deal, and the power to expand her career in any way she chooses. Lindsay has admitted that she would love to go to school to study law or fashion one day, but right now higher education plans are on hold. "I definitely plan to go to college at some point, but not right now," she told the *Edmonton Sun*. "It's important I establish myself as an actor before I take time off. To go to college now would be to put on hold everything I've been working toward so hard these past couple of years."

Lindsay is determined to focus on developing her two talents—acting and singing—so she can keep receiving critical acclaim and respect. She has been approached about putting her name on things like fashion lines (her peers Mary-Kate and Ashley Olsen and Hilary Duff all have their own lines), but Lindsay just doesn't think that's a path she wants to take. "The actresses I look up to and admire—like Audrey Hepburn, Marilyn Monroe, Ann-Margret, all these women I love and aspire to be like—they never did clothing lines," Lindsay told *Seventeen* magazine. "Jodie Foster didn't. Julia Roberts didn't. I want to follow what they've done in my own way."

And while Lindsay is looking forward to growing with her audience and taking on more serious roles as she gets older, it's very important to Lindsay that she pace herself and not grow up ahead of her fans. "I want to branch out and find edgier stuff, but I just don't think now is the right time. I have to find the right script before I do anything just to do it," she told MTV.com. And there is one genre you definitely won't see Lindsay in: anything that is remotely scary. "I don't want to do horror or movies with killers in them," Lindsay told the New York *Daily News*. "I'll try to stick to happy movies."

No matter what the genre, Lindsay is committed to choosing roles that will give her the opportunity to try new things. As she told *Interview* magazine, "I want to act more. I want to really act in a film and commit to something and be a different person. I mean, the characters I've played so far are very similar to who I am, so it's hard to say that I'm actually fully acting. I want to find something that's a little bit more dramatic, something that's different from what I usually do. I don't want to give an image of doing only teen movies and just being this perfect teen."

While we're on the subject of her megawatt future, Lindsay has six incredible movies she's working on right now. Here's a sneak peek:

Herbie: Fully Loaded. More than twenty years ago, there was a series of popular movies about Herbie, a Volkswagen Bug that could drive itself. In this new installment, Herbie gets into the world of NASCAR racing. Lindsay actually has to take NASCAR driving lessons to prepare for the flick!

Dramarama. Lindsay plays a star actress in the drama program at a prestigious private high school. When her parents have to scale back their luxurious lifestyle, they enroll Lindsay's character in public school. Acting is her calling, so she wastes no time forming a drama club at her new school and then takes on her old classmates in a drama competition.

Gossip Girl. In this movie (based on the popular series of young adult novels), Lindsay will star as Blair Waldorf, the most popular girl on Manhattan's Upper East Side. But Blair's perfect world crumbles when her archenemy returns to New York after getting expelled from boarding school.

Love and Death at Terrington Prep. Lindsay is in negotiations to star in this dark, independent film. It is the edgiest and riskiest role that Lindsay has been considered for yet. The details of this drama about the lives of private school kids are still top secret, but one thing that *has* been revealed is Lindsay's amazing costar. It's none other than *The O.C.*'s Adam Brody!

Fashionistas. Lindsay is set to star in this film about a fashion student who dreams of becoming a designer. According to *Variety,* Lindsay will executive produce the project as well as act!

Lady Luck. Daily Variety also reports that Lindsay is in final negotiations to star in this upcoming comedy about what happens when the luckiest girl in the world meets a perennial loser and gains his bad luck instead. Lindsay will earn a whopping $7.5 million paycheck for this film—talk about luck!

If there is one thing you can say about Lindsay it's that she loves to keep busy. She may have a ton on her plate right now, but she intends to space out her music and movie career to guarantee that she will be around for a long, long time. As she told *Seventeen*, "I don't think it's a smart idea for anybody to do everything at once, because then you have nowhere to go—there is no mystery about you and nothing to get to know." Well, we are certainly looking forward to getting to know more about her in the future!

Chapter 12

•

Lindsay's "It" List

Here's a quick Lindsay cheat sheet:

Birthdate: July 2, 1986
Sign: Cancer

Parents: Dina and Michael
Siblings: Aliana, Michael, and Dakota

Eye Color: Green
Hair: Auburn

Favorite Color: Pink
Favorite Food: Japanese

Best Subjects: Math and science

Hobbies: Swimming, skating, biking, reading, writing

Shoe size: Nine

Favorite Movies:
Pretty Woman
Ferris Bueller's Day Off
The Little Mermaid
All I Wanna Do
Bring It On
Heartbreakers

Favorite TV Shows:
Friends
Gilmore Girls
7th Heaven
Dawson's Creek

Favorite Actresses:
Julia Roberts
Sandra Bullock
Jennifer Aniston
Jodie Foster
Audrey Hepburn
Ann-Margret

Favorite Music: "I love Outkast. Their CD *Speakerboxx/The Love Below* is so great. Both of them are so cool. And I love Liz Phair," Lindsay said during an interview on the *Mean Girls* set.

Favorite Album: *The Immaculate Collection,* by Madonna. "I'm a huge Madonna fan. My favorite song is 'Material Girl,'" Lindsay revealed in *People* magazine.

Favorite Peer in the Industry: "Evan Rachel Wood. She's so talented that she's separated herself from everyone else," Lindsay told *Interview* magazine.

Pet Peeve: "People who talk with food in their mouths and chew real loud," she admitted in *J-14.* Also "denim on denim," she told *Your Prom* magazine.

Celebrity Love: Johnny Depp (FYI: Lindsay wanted to try out for his upcoming movie, a remake of *Willie Wonka and the Chocolate Factory,* but she was too old.)

Celebrity Crushes: Orlando Bloom and Colin Farrell

Won't Leave Home Without: Her cell phone

Bedtime: One a.m.

Beauty Must-Have: Chap Stick

Favorite Designer: Christian Dior

Catch Phrase: Peace and Love

Car: Mercedes Benz

Biggest Splurge: An $80,000 Chopard watch. "It's covered in diamonds," Lindsay said in *People*.

Personal Style: "My style changes all the time. It might be jeans with stilettos, or a little skirt with a Chrome Hearts tank top and a pair of Uggs," Lindsay told *Your Prom* magazine.

Favorite Junk Food: McDonald's Happy Meals

Guilty Pleasure: *American Idol*. "I love that show. I think it's great. I feel bad though, because the judges are really mean sometimes. I could never do that. I can't just be mean to people. Some people are horrible, but they know what they're getting themselves into—they just go there and audition as a joke," Lindsay said in *J-14*.

Dream Prom Date: Eminem. "He's not even that good looking! It's his voice!" Lindsay revealed in *Your Prom*.

Chapter 13

•

Lindsay Gets Personal

Lindsay has an opinion, a funny story, or a bit of advice on almost every topic. Here are the best quotes, personal stories, fun memories, and words of wisdom that Lindsay has shared:

THAT'S HOLLYWOOD

ROLE REVERSAL: "Madonna. I would switch roles with Madonna for a day. Or if Audrey Hepburn were still alive, Audrey Hepburn. I love Audrey Hepburn. She's one of my idols also," Lindsay said during an interview on the set of *Mean Girls*.

MISSING JULIA (ROBERTS, THAT IS): "I went to the premiere for *Anywhere but Here* with my mom. While we were driving on the street, we saw Julia Roberts! I told my mom to stop the car, but I got too embarrassed so we drove away! Julia Roberts is one of my favorite actresses, so I'm regretting it to this day," Lindsay told *Teen Celebrity*.

GOOD BODY IMAGE: "People I admire, like Marilyn Monroe and Audrey Hepburn and Ann-Margret, had beautiful figures. I don't like the fact that people my age are dealing with today's images, because they're not realistic and people think that's how they should be presenting themselves. It's scary because these little kids are looking at you like you're perfect, and nobody's perfect. If you're willing to grow up in public, then you have to be yourself," Lindsay said in *Seventeen*.

THE SEXY LIFE: "Personally, I think it would be nice if the studios went back to how they used to be when they protected their actresses—and girls wore more clothing. That may sound hypocritical because I like to wear sexy things sometimes, but that's just because the only things that people consider sexy right now is what's out there. If sexy was brought back in the way that Marilyn Monroe or Brigitte Bardot used to do it, then it might be different," Lindsay told *Interview*.

LIFE'S DEFINING MOMENTS

MOST EMBARRASSING: Lindsay said to *Popstar*: "I was with a friend at a movie theater. She was talking to this guy she had a crush on. And we were walking and I went to kick her from the side, and I got caught in this guy's pants, because they were kind of baggy, and I flew forward and everything in my purse came flying out all over the place and I fell flat on my face! It was a really crowded movie theater and everybody saw me."

FIRST KISS: "It was with someone that I really liked and I guess that's all that matters. I was in the eighth grade and he was in the ninth. It was the first few weeks back at school, at a friend's house. I was so nervous about it. And it's just weird because you think, 'Is he going to do it? Am I? When do I stop?' You know? It's awkward," she said in *Popstar*.

THE 411 ON DATING

THREE THINGS YOU SHOULD NEVER FORGET ON A DATE: "Gum, your cell phone, and cash. Cash because I'm not the kind of girl that waits for a guy to, like, take out his wallet and pay," Lindsay revealed in *Popstar*.

BEST DATING ADVICE: "Don't take anything too seriously. There's a lot of game playing and I hate that. And you have to really trust the person. Be yourself. Don't change yourself for anyone. And just have fun with the whole thing!" Lindsay told *Popstar*.

BEST DATE SPOT: Lindsay said in *Popstar*: "I think going to the beach with someone is a little more intimate than anything else. The movies are really awkward because, actually, I went on a date with someone that I really liked to the movies and you want to talk to them but you can't talk to them. And there's always that thing of like, 'Is it annoying if I talk during the movie and ask something?'"

GROWING UP

OVERCOMING A BAD RAP: "I don't know what the Hollywood rules are exactly, but I don't like them. For instance, I had friends in town recently on spring break. They wanted to go out every night and I wanted to show them a good time. So I took them out and the paparazzi started taking pictures of me and then called my publicist and said, 'We're going to write a story on her, and we're going to call her the new "it party girl."' Just because I'm seventeen and I'm having fun, they start saying I'm trying to be older, partying and going crazy. I don't even like to drink!" Lindsay told *Interview* magazine.

FRIENDSHIP BLUES: "Someone I hadn't spoken to in years, ever since *The Parent Trap*—she was in it with me—called me and said, 'Hey, I heard you got a movie. Do you want to meet up?' And she hadn't called me in five years. So it was just kind of weird and it's like, 'I know why you're calling me,'" Lindsay said in *Popstar.*

THE FRIENDSHIP TEST: "I don't want this to sound obnoxious or anything, but I feel like I'm one of the best friends anyone could have. I'm really loyal because that's all I look for in a friend. All I want is somebody I can trust and who will be there for me," Lindsay told *Popstar.*

POWER TRIP: "I've been working hard and trying to get to this position, and I feel like people are starting to recognize the stuff that I'm doing, and enjoying it.

It makes me feel really good when my little sister and her friends peek inside my bedroom door and stare at me. It's cool to have people look up to you. But I'm not in a position yet where I can just be like, 'Oh, I want to do this kind of movie,'" Lindsay said in *Interview* magazine.

HIGH SCHOOL ADVICE

ON LEAVING HIGH SCHOOL: Lindsay told *J-14*: "I don't miss leaving and coming back to school all the time. It's hard to leave my friends and not know what's going on at school. There is so much drama in high school and I just couldn't do it anymore. It affects me when I'm working because I get stressed out and tired on set, so I couldn't deal with that too. It's easier for me to just get my work done for school here and then see my friends separately."

ON DEALING WITH MEAN GIRLS: "I think when you say something back to someone who's speaking badly of you, it's just going to drag the whole thing out. I would say just be completely nice to them and kill them with kindness. Then they'll be like, 'Why are they being so nice to me?' and they won't know what to say back. I am a very honest person to begin with.

So if someone is going to say something to me, I just let it go. That freaks people out because they want to fight sometimes. It's usually over in a week anyway, so why waste time fighting about it?" Lindsay said in an interview on the set of *Mean Girls*.

AVOIDING THE DRAMA: "Girls like drama. It gives them something to do in high school. It's enjoyable to get involved with drama . . . but then when you get older, it's kind of a hassle. It's just not something that's fun to deal with. Don't talk about someone behind their back, because they'll find out eventually," Lindsay said on CNN.com.

LISTEN TO MOM AND DAD: "Adults have been through high school and that's something for them to look back on and teach their kids to help them through it," Lindsay said on CNN.com.

Chapter 14

•

Lindsay Goes First

Lindsay's desire to succeed and be a star has everything to do with her incredible talent. But being the oldest of four actually had a little something to do with it too. Studies show that firstborn children typically grow up to be natural leaders and high achievers. They tend to love the spotlight and know how to make things happen. Lindsay knew at only three years old that she wanted to be in the movies. Today, not only is she an actress, but she's also a full-fledged star. Not too shabby!

Firstborn children are precise and pay close

attention to detail. They always give one hundred percent because they want things done right the first time. Ever since Lindsay was a child, her costars have complimented her for being mature and always learning her lines on time. Lindsay isn't satisfied unless she completes every scene to perfection. She has developed a great relationship with every director she's worked with. They truly appreciate the interest she takes in each role she plays and the way she always puts all of her energy into the film.

Lindsay's relationship with her mom and dad is unique because she was their first child. When Lindsay was born, parenting was new and exciting for them. They wanted her to succeed and set a good example for the younger children. Lindsay definitely met those expectations and then some with her amazing career, and she credits much of her success to the close relationship she has with her mother and father. They've supported Lindsay's career since she was three years old, even traveling as far as London for her to make movies. They never urged Lindsay to sign on to a film she wasn't sure about, and they made sure she stayed grounded and appreciated the amazing opportunities she was offered. When Lindsay decided she wanted to go back to school after she made *The Parent Trap,* her parents stood by her. "It was a gamble for me as a mom because I didn't want her to grow up hating me," Lindsay's mom, Dina, told the *Los Angeles Times.* "If she stayed in Hollywood, she'd be a nightmare now. Kids need boundaries." So when Lindsay felt she was old enough to start acting again full-time, her parents gave her their blessing without hesitation. Lindsay's parents trusted that their first-born daughter was making the right decisions for herself. And by doing so, they helped Lindsay make all of her dreams come true.

Children who are born first receive a lot of extra attention, because in their family they're first to do, well, everything! They're the first to be toilet trained, first to date, first to drive a car. Then there are the younger siblings who look up to them and want to be just like them. That was certainly the case in the Lohan household. Lindsay's siblings were all very much in awe of her modeling and acting career. Lindsay loves having their support, and whenever possible she arranges for them to appear as extras in her movies.

Lindsay has two brothers she's extremely close with, but her relationship with her sister, Aliana, is special. Aliana truly idolizes her big sister. "My sister tries to be like me," Lindsay told *Girl's Life* magazine. "I don't mind because she's really cute the way she does it. A lot of what I do, I do for my sister." Being away from Aliana when she's off making movies is hard for Lindsay, and now that she lives in L.A. instead of with her family in New York, it's even more difficult. On the set of *Mean Girls* Lindsay revealed, "I try to go home and visit my family as much as possible. I was home for two hours before I had to go to the city and work, and my sister was like, 'You know what? I don't even consider you my sister anymore.' That killed me. I was like, 'What?' And she was like, 'You are never here!' She's so funny, but we did talk about it later because it's hard to leave home and then come back and leave my family again."

Chapter 15

Written in the Stars

Born on July 2, 1986, Lindsay's astrological sign is Cancer (June 22 to July 23). Here's everything you need to know about what makes Cancers tick:

Cancers are generally emotional, loving, intuitive, imaginative, protective, and sympathetic. Sounds like Lindsay, right? She's in touch with her emotions, which helps make her such a great actress. She is open and giving to her family and friends. (Lindsay always credits her success to the amazing group of people she was surrounded by while growing up.) And she's taken her career to an enormously successful level by following her heart.

As a typical Cancer, Lindsay has always stayed true to herself and trusted her gut when making decisions that she knew could affect her career. When she wanted to go back to school after *The Parent Trap,* Lindsay instinctively knew it was the right thing to do. Another young actor with such a promising career may have been too nervous to leave acting behind for fear of never finding another chance to get back into the business. But Lindsay knew deep down that if acting was her destiny, it would be waiting for her to go back to whenever she was ready.

Cancers love living in a comfortable home where they can invite friends and family over. Lindsay says that the apartment she shared with Raven was filled with people all the time because she "needed to be with friends." Lindsay even admits that she gets scared when she's home alone!

Sometimes to the outside world Cancers appear to be thick-skinned. It may seem like nothing bothers them, but usually they're just hiding their feelings to protect themselves. Lindsay's a pro at keeping her emotions locked inside when things are going on in her personal life. She needs to be guarded if she doesn't want the press to catch wind and write about her problems. But even though Cancers are good at hiding their emotions in public, behind closed doors they love expressing to their friends and family how much they appreciate and need their love and support. Lindsay leans on her loved ones when things get crazy and depends on them to help her through the rough patches. Therefore it makes perfect sense that Cancers are known for being extremely loyal friends who give without asking for much in return.

When it comes to choosing the perfect career for a Cancer, believe it or not, acting tops the list! Cancers have overactive imaginations and are passionate about art and literature and feel right at home on the stage. They love daydreaming and fantasizing about how they can make those dreams a reality. That fits Lindsay to a T—every night before bed she used to pray that she could be an actress in a movie.

It certainly looks like Lindsay's acting career was written in the stars!

Chapter 16

•

We've Got Lindsay's Number

Being the firstborn child in her family and a Cancer are hints that Lindsay was destined to be a famous actress. But there is one more piece to the puzzle that makes up Lindsay's star power (besides hard work and talent, of course) that is found in the deeper meaning behind her name.

In the ancient science of numerology, it is believed that the letters of your name each correspond to a number. If you add all those numbers up and then keep reducing them until you get a number between one and nine, you can learn a great deal about your personality. So, let's find Lindsay's number and then you can look up yours, too!

Lindsay may be a perfect ten in your eyes, but according to numerology, she is a four. So what does that mean? Fours don't like to live life in a hurry. They are practical, stable, hardworking, and faithful to those around them. We know that Lindsay has worked harder than most eighteen-year-olds to get to where she is today. And it goes without saying that she is a loyal friend, actress, and daughter.

Let's examine how to calculate Lindsay's number. Write out all the letters of the name (full name only—no nicknames—including first, middle, and last) and match the letters to the number they correspond to using the chart below.

```
1 2 3 4 5 6 7 8 9
A B C D E F G H I
J K L M N O P Q R
S T U V W X Y Z
```

Here's how we figured out Lindsay's name:

```
L I N D S A Y   M O R G A N   L O H A N
3 9 5 4 1 1 7   4 6 9 7 1 5   3 6 8 1 5
```

When we added all the numbers together we got 85. But numerology only works between the numbers one and nine. So we added 8 and 5 together to equal 13. Then we added 1 and 3 together to find Lindsay's magical number of 4!

When you add up the numbers of your own name, use the guide below to see what your personal number means. Maybe you're a four like Lindsay—and if not, maybe you'll discover you have something in common with her in your own unique way.

One: This is considered the head of all the Cosmos. You love attention and are a natural born leader.

Two: You're a follower instead of a leader because you don't want to hurt anyone's feelings. You love the art of good conversation and always take both sides of a story into consideration.

Three: You have many talents and love creativity and imagination. You use your talent to better the world.

Four: Well, one thing is for sure—you and Lindsay are soul sisters!

Five: You hate having nothing to do, so you're

always on the go. You love being around people and you have tons of energy. If you're bored, it won't be long before you find adventure.

Six: You are romantic, peaceful, and devoted to your family. Sixes love to create art and music or write.

Seven: You may keep to yourself, but that's because you're always thinking, dreaming, and analyzing.

Eight: You are hardworking and determined. Eights are outspoken and opinionated but extremely loyal to everyone in their life.

Nine: You are all about the good and welfare of humanity. Nines are on a quest to save the world.

Chapter 17

•

How Well Do You *Really* Know Lindsay?

Answer these true/false questions and see how "true" a Lindsay fan you really are!

1. Lindsay's mom was a Dallas Cowboys Cheerleader.
2. Lindsay dated pop singer Aaron Carter.
3. In *The Parent Trap*, Lindsay plays triplets.
4. Lindsay's favorite cuisine is Japanese.
5. Lindsay says her favorite commercial she made was for Swiss Miss pudding.
6. The movie Lindsay starred in with Tyra Banks was called *Life-Size*.

7. Lindsay was in one episode of a TV show with Bette Midler.

8. Lindsay appeared on shopping bags for the Gap.

9. Lindsay says Outkast is one of her favorite groups.

10. Lindsay did not contribute a song to the *Freaky Friday* sound track.

11. *Mean Girls* was based on a book.

12. *Mean Girls* was written by *Saturday Night Live* star Molly Shannon.

13. Chad Michael Murray plays Lindsay's love interest in *Freaky Friday*.

14. Kelly Osbourne was supposed to star in *Freaky Friday* with Lindsay but dropped out before shooting began.

15. Lindsay appeared on the soap opera *General Hospital*.

16. Lindsay was roommates in Los Angeles with actress Raven.

17. Lindsay grew up in Connecticut.

18. Lindsay has two younger sisters.

19. Lindsay left high school in eleventh grade.

20. Lindsay cites one of her beauty must-haves as Chap Stick.

21. Lindsay has been feuding with actress Hilary Duff.
22. Lindsay is going to star in a movie with James Lafferty from the TV show *One Tree Hill*.
23. Lindsay is going to star in the next installment of the Herbie the Love Bug movies for Disney.
24. Lindsay played the drums in *Freaky Friday*.
25. Lindsay's costar in *Confessions of a Teenage Drama Queen* was rising star Alison Pill.
26. Lindsay has a crush on actor Johnny Depp.
27. Lindsay's upcoming movie *Gossip Girl* is based on a book.
28. Lindsay appeared on *The Mickey Mouse Club* with Britney Spears.
29. Lindsay is recording her first music album.
30. Lindsay had her own sitcom on Nickelodeon.

The Answers
1. False
2. True
3. False
4. True
5. False
6. True
7. True
8. False
9. True
10. False
11. True
12. False
13. True
14. True
15. False
16. True
17. False
18. False
19. True
20. True
21. True
22. False
23. True
24. False
25. True
26. True
27. True
28. False
29. True
30. False

Lindsay's Career Timeline

1996 *Another World* (TV series) . . . . Alli Fowler
1998 *The Parent Trap* . . . . Hallie Parker/Annie James
2000 *Life-Size* (TV) . . . . Casey
2000 *Bette* (TV series) . . . . Rose
2002 *Get a Clue* (TV) . . . . Lexy Gold
2003 *Freaky Friday* . . . . Anna Coleman
2004 *Confessions of a Teenage Drama Queen* . . . . Lola
2004 *Mean Girls* . . . . Cady Heron

In Production

Dramarama
Gossip Girl
Herbie: Fully Loaded
Love and Death at Tarrington Prep
Fashionistas
Lady Luck

Chapter 18

•

Let's Go Surfing

If you can't get to the movies to see Lindsay light up the big screen or you can't find her anywhere on TV, we have the perfect way for you to get your Lindsay Lohan fix any time of the day or night. Just turn on your computer and you can find a whole world of Web sites devoted to your favorite redhead, keep up with the latest news, and even interact with other fans who are just as crazy about Lindsay as you are! Sound fun? Get ready to start clicking on these awesome Web sites!

Lindsay Lohan's Official Web Site
www.llrocks.com

**The Official Lindsay Lohan Fan Site—
by her fans, for her fans**
www.lindsayfans.com

Loving Lindsay
www.lovinglindsay.50megs.com

The Lindsay Lohan Community
lindsaylohan.com

Lindsay Fan
www.lindsay-lohan.org

LOHANonline
www.lohanonline.com

Internet Movie Database
www.imdb.com/name/nm0517820